ECHOSTAR

Published by Barrington Stoke
An imprint of HarperCollins*Publishers*
Westerhill Road, Bishopbriggs, Glasgow, G64 2QT

www.barringtonstoke.co.uk

HarperCollins*Publishers*
Macken House, 39/40 Mayor Street Upper,
Dublin 1, DO1 C9W8, Ireland

First published in 2024

Text © 2024 Melinda Salisbury
Cover design and illustration © 2024 Holly Ovenden

The moral right of Melinda Salisbury to be identified
as the author of this work has been asserted in accordance
with the Copyright, Designs and Patents Act, 1988

ISBN 978-1-80090-270-1

10 9 8 7 6 5 4 3 2 1

A catalogue record for this book is available from the British Library

Printed and Bound in the UK using 100% Renewable Electricity
at Martins the Printers Ltd

ECHOSTAR

IS ALWAYS LISTENING

MELINDA SALISBURY

Barrington Stoke

CHAPTER 1

I skidded into the seat beside Deva, my best friend, as the last ring of the bell faded away into a tense, expectant silence. It was a feat so impossible, so *miraculous*, it should be turned into a film, starring me, written, directed and produced by me. It was cinematic. It was spectacular. It was—

"Disgraceful," said Mrs McGinty, my Biology teacher, as she glared at me. "Truly, Ruby. Disgraceful. When the bell rings, you should already be in your seat with your books out for the start of the lesson, not hurling yourself across the room like an animal," she continued.

"I'm sorry, Miss," I replied, offering a winning smile. "What can I say? I live for the drama."

A few people laughed, and Mrs McGinty's expression darkened into a dangerous look.

It was a look I knew well.

I braced myself, determined to go to the guillotine with my head held high (at least while it was still attached). But somehow, instead of giving me detention, Mrs McGinty exhaled slowly and opened the register.

"Thank you, Universe," I muttered.

"I thought you were toast this time," Deva said. "Where were you?"

"Asking about the end-of-year show," I said, glancing at Mrs McGinty, who was calling out names. "I made it clear to Mr Conti I'm ready for an actual speaking role this year. You'd think he'd realise I have star quality."

"Ruby Brookes," Mrs McGinty barked.

I snapped my head around. "Here, Miss."

"We all know you're here, Ruby," Mrs McGinty said. "We can hear you whispering to Miss Shah."

I held up my hands as I couldn't deny it, and everyone laughed again.

Mrs McGinty blinked, then went back to the register. I mouthed, "To be continued," at

Deva and opened my exercise book, fighting back a yawn.

Biology was not my best subject. Neither was Chemistry. Or Physics. Or Maths, English, English Lit., Geography, French, History or PE. I was so-so at Art, as long as my teachers let me embrace my inner Picasso. With still life and classic portraits, I was somewhat less gifted.

I really did live for Drama.

Standing on stage in the spotlight was the only time I felt like myself. It was ironic, considering I was pretending to be someone else. My first word was apparently "star" – my parents thought I was talking about the shape, but I know I was talking about my destiny.

I wanted to be in films: I'd start as an indie darling and become a Hollywood icon. In TV, there would be a couple of cameos in crime shows followed by a lead role in something award-winning. But most important of all was appearing on stage. Repertory, Off-Broadway, on Broadway, a West End transfer. I needed an audience. I needed—

"—to pay attention!" growled Mrs McGinty.

Deva elbowed me in the arm.

I looked up to find our teacher towering over us, her eyes bulging like a frog's.

"Well?" she demanded.

"Sorry, Miss. Could you repeat the question? If there was a question."

I thought she was going to explode. Her face was the colour of an aubergine.

Deva rescued me, saying, "The four bases that make up DNA are T, A, G and C."

I stared at Deva.

Mrs McGinty was also staring at her.

Deva pushed her glasses up her nose. "I think," she added.

"That's right, Miss Shah," Mrs McGinty said, blinking. "Well done. Your work has been very impressive this term. I'm glad to see at least one of you putting in the effort. Keep it up."

Deva gave a small nod.

Mrs McGinty smiled at her, scowled at me and went back to the front of the room.

"Read the chapter on DNA bases and then answer the questions I'm going to write on the board. You don't need to talk while you're reading," Mrs McGinty added, glaring at me.

The moment she looked away, I turned to Deva to ask how she suddenly knew about DNA bases and why old McGinty thought her work was impressive – Deva used to be as bad at Biology as me. Then I paused. I didn't want to get either of us into any more trouble. Instead, I tore a page from the middle of my exercise book and scribbled on it, sliding it along the table to Deva.

What does she mean your work has been impressive this term? Are you blackmailing her?

Deva looked at my note, adjusted her glasses and jotted a short reply, pushing it back to me.

I've been studying, she'd written.

I mock gasped at Deva, clutching an imaginary pearl necklace. *Are you possessed?* I wrote back.

Deva shrugged, her pen moving quickly. *My mum says I can't go to the ATF Camp if I don't sort my grades out.*

I sucked in a sharp breath. Deva and I had both been offered free places at the Ash Tree Foundation Performing Arts Camp this summer after auditioning earlier in the year.

It sounded amazing: six weeks of workshops and classes and talks with real showbiz professionals. They hadn't revealed who yet, but there were rumours about some of the tutors they'd hired – and they were big. *Hollywood* big. Agents and scouts too. Deva and I had been dreaming of summer ever since.

My mum said the same, I replied. *But there's no way she means it.*

My mum means it, Deva wrote.

Deva pulled the paper back and added something else before I could reply.

I need to concentrate. Talk at lunch.

She slid the page over to me and then bent over her book, pushing her glasses up her nose as her dark hair spilled onto the desk.

I tried to focus on my own work, but I could almost feel the words going in through my eyes and then slinking straight out of my ears without ever going near my memory. It wasn't that I had a terrible memory – give me a monologue, and I'd have it down in twenty-four hours. Biology stuff wouldn't stick because it was boring, and I'd never been good at paying attention to things I found boring.

I was still reading the first page of the DNA chapter when Deva started writing.

From the corner of my eye, I saw her pen whipping across her exercise book as she worked through the questions on the board. She wasn't even pausing to think, as if she already knew what the answers were.

I got so caught up in watching her that when the bell went for the end of the lesson, I jumped, startled by the sound. I hadn't even finished the reading, let alone started the questions.

"All right, make a note of anything you haven't answered yet and complete it for your homework," Mrs McGinty declared. Everyone was shoving their books and pencil cases into their bags. "I'll expect it next lesson."

I groaned and rushed to copy down everything on the board.

"I'll give them to you," Deva offered.

"Thanks, you're a—"

I lunged over to hug Deva and accidentally knocked her glasses off.

"No!" Deva cried. She scrabbled to pick them up from under my seat where they'd landed, but I'd already got them.

"They're OK," I said, examining them. "Not broken. Oh, hang on, there's something caught—"

Before I could finish, Deva snatched the glasses from my hand, smoothing a long, transparent string down along one of the arms. She looked at the front carefully, then put them on, tucking the string *inside* her ear and pulling her hair over to hide it.

She wouldn't look at me.

"What is that?" I asked.

"Not here," Deva whispered.

"Deva—"

"Ruby, please."

Then Deva met my eyes.

She was terrified. I'd never seen her like this before, not even just before performing in a show.

I got stage fright, but Deva never did. She was always cool, always calm.

"Please," Deva said again.

I nodded, a twisting sensation in my stomach.

Something was very, very wrong.

Deva jerked her head towards the door, then began to walk away. After a second, I followed, my mind racing, my heart pounding.

We were the only two in our form who brought lunch from home. It meant we had the form room to ourselves until everyone else finished in the cafeteria.

"Dev, you're scaring me," I said as soon as we were safely inside, the door shut firmly behind us.

Deva closed her eyes, like she was in pain, and my stomach lurched again.

"If I tell you, you have to swear not to tell anyone else. Or get mad," Deva said.

"Why would I get mad?" I asked.

Deva pulled her phone out of her pocket, unlocking it. A few seconds later, she handed it to me.

An app was open on the screen.

"What's *EchoStar*?" I asked.

CHAPTER 2

Deva took a deep breath.

"It's an app to help people know what to say – especially people who have social anxiety," she said.

I frowned. "Since when do you have social anxiety?"

"I don't." Deva paused and licked her lips. "*EchoStar* gives you answers to things the AI sees and hears when you have it turned on. It was originally designed to help people in social situations, but you can use it for other stuff."

"How does it work?" I asked. Then I realised. "It's the string on your glasses," I said. "It's an earpiece? No way!"

Deva nodded. "There's a microphone." She tapped the corner of her glasses by the hinge, and

I moved closer. "And a camera. It can see and respond to written things too."

They were tiny black bumps on the edges of her glasses frame, and one was connected to the wire. Even up close they looked like part of the design.

"Wow," I said, sitting back. "They're so tiny."

"Apparently, they were developed by MI6, and they're still classified technology," Deva said. "The whole app is based on spy tech – like when they put a wire on you in films and someone feeds you lines."

"From a person?" I asked.

Deva shook her head. "No, it's all AI. It runs via an app on your phone and transmits the data to the AI database. The AI analyses what it hears or sees and tells you what to say and write. It's really good if you can't think of what to say."

"But you're using it to cheat," I said.

My words echoed around the empty classroom.

"It's not that bad," Deva said. Her expression was defiant as she looked back at me. "I don't use it all the time. I can't – there's a delay while it thinks of a reply. Only a little one, but still. And sometimes the AI goes offline for updating and I'm stuck with just my brain. Or the AI glitches and says weird things and I have to restart it. I couldn't use it in an exam or anything. And I wouldn't," Deva added firmly. "It's only for now. My mum says as long as I get sixes or above, then I can go to ATF Camp, and that's all I need it for. After that, I'm done with *EchoStar*."

I couldn't keep the hurt from my voice as I said, "How long have you had it? Why didn't you tell me about it?"

"Just since the start of term. And I couldn't tell you. I'd promised I wouldn't," Deva said.

"What do you mean, *promised*?"

Deva glanced at the closed door nervously, swallowing before she said, "I had to sign an NDA swearing I wouldn't talk about it. Because of the tech, and because I'm using a super-beta version as part of the testing. You can't get it in the app store."

I didn't understand. "If it's so secret, how did you find out about it?"

Deva blushed, her brown cheeks darkening.

"They approached me," she said. "I was looking up studying advice online. How to get better at school, stuff like that." She gave a small, embarrassed laugh, then continued.

"Rubes, my mum is dead serious about not letting me go to ATF Camp if I don't sort my grades out. She's talking about me giving up dancing so it doesn't distract me from exams. I need to get an actual professional dancer to tell her I've got what it takes to go all the way and really make a living from it. She might listen to them."

I understood completely.

Deva and I met when we were ten and a film was being made in our town. The casting people had sent notices to all the schools, inviting pupils to be film extras during half-term. I'd convinced my mum I would die if she didn't take me. On the first day, I'd met Deva, who was there with her dance school. Her teacher was friends with one of the producers.

By the end of the week, we were best friends, and I was thrilled when it turned out we would be going to the same senior school. I liked Deva so much I wasn't even angry when they cut my scene from the film but kept hers. Sometimes at sleepovers we'd put it on and pause it on the split second you can see Deva leaping across the stage in the background of the final scene. She looks like she's flying.

So, I got it. I knew what dancing meant to her, and she was right – if we did well at ATF Camp, both of us might be able to start our dream careers in the industry before we were even sixteen. We'd make contacts at the very least, which was just as important.

But by cheating to get there? I wasn't sure.

Deva hid behind her hands, then continued.

"Please don't judge me, but after a billion videos and preachy blog posts about studying, I went a bit wild and asked on a tech forum if anyone knew of anything. This guy said he might have a way to help, and to message him about it if I was serious. I guessed he was going to send nudes, because *the internet*, but I decided to risk it. And he sent the link to the *EchoStar* app." Deva lowered her hands and looked at me.

"What about the earpiece and the camera?" I said. "Where did they come from?"

She pulled a face. "I ... gave him my address."

"Are you serious?" I yelled, ignoring her when she flapped at me to make me stop. "You gave your address to a random man online so he could send you equipment that works with his special app that you can't tell anyone about? Deva, do you hear yourself?"

The classroom door opened and Mr Kimura, our form tutor, peered around it.

"Everything OK, girls?" he asked. "Are you rehearsing for something, Ruby?"

Deva turned to me, her eyes wide and pleading, and I switched into character.

"Always, Mr K," I replied.

He gave a tired smile. "Do you think maybe you can rehearse more quietly?"

"You got it, Sir. Sorry," I said.

"Break a leg," Mr Kimura replied, and closed the door.

"I know it was a risk," Deva said, before I could start ranting again. "But you understand why I had to, right? You are the only person in the world who knows what this means to me. To us."

I sighed.

Deva reached for my hand and took it. "I'm just going to do it until our end-of-year reports get sent home. Then my mum will be happy, she'll let me go to the camp and our futures as stars will begin."

Her phone lit up, and Deva beamed.

"The new Conrad O'Connell video just dropped. Shall we?"

I rolled my eyes and replied, "The day just keeps getting better."

Deva gave me a look. "You just need to watch his stuff more."

"I'd rather dig my eyes out with a rusty fork."

"He'll grow on you," Deva said as she unlocked her phone and opened the video app.

"Like a fungus?"

"Hush and look at the pretty boy talking."

Deva shoved her phone in my face, and that was the end of the conversation about *EchoStar*.

*

Or at least I'd thought it was.

I got home from school and found out Mrs Owusu, our head of year, had decided to email midterm reports of our projected grades to our parents. The reports highlighted *"opportunities for us to improve"* before the final reports were made. Mrs Owusu said this was a good thing, as the final reports went on our permanent records but the midterm ones didn't.

My midterm report showed I had a LOT of opportunities to improve. In fact, all I had were opportunities to improve. I was getting twos and threes in almost everything except Drama. I had a nine in Drama.

I had a one in Biology.

"Ruby, this isn't good enough," Mum said. "You're starting your GCSEs next year. This is crunch time."

My mum's hands were on her hips, her green eyes blazing. I wasn't used to my mother being home when I got back from school. She ran a catering company, a pretty good one, but that meant she was out a lot. I had the house to myself most of the time.

"Mum, it's a projection of grades. It's not real. I have time to fix it. It's going to be fine. *'There is no following her in this fierce vein,'*" I quoted.

"Is that from a play?" Mum asked, answering her own question a second later by adding, "Of course it is. You know, if you spent half as much time trying to remember equations as you do memorising dead men's words, you'd be doing a lot better."

"Shakespeare is on the curriculum, Mum."

Her eyes blazed again, her face pinching. I knew I'd gone too far.

"You know what?" Mum said. "Seeing as Drama is the only thing that you're doing well at, maybe you don't need to go to a summer camp for it. Maybe I should find you a camp for sciences."

"No—" I started to say.

"Yes, Ruby. Pull up your grades or you are not going to the Ash Tree Foundation Camp. I mean it."

CHAPTER 3

Deva had promised not to tell anyone about *EchoStar*, so I couldn't ask her to put me in touch with the guy who'd given it to her.

But I needed it now too.

I paced my bedroom, racking my brain for a way to get it. Deva hadn't said which forum she'd been on, and I couldn't ask her without it looking suspicious, especially as I was so against it earlier. The only idea I had was to post on *every* forum I could think of and hope her guy found me like he found her.

Then I stopped, slapping my own forehead. What was I thinking? I needed to do what Miss Albright was always telling us in Computer Science and "*optimise my search terms*". I threw myself onto my bed and opened my laptop.

The advantage to being super-best friends with someone was that you knew what their username was, even on the accounts they didn't want their parents to find. Deva's "official" accounts were all under *TheDevaDShah*, but on her real accounts – the ones she actually used – she went by *ChoreoManiac*.

I opened the browser and typed "*ChoreoManiac, help at school*" into the search bar. Then, after a moment's thought, I added "*desperate*" and hit return.

It was the top result. I punched the air before opening the page.

It was exactly like she'd said: Deva asking for help, and a few recommendations for online video courses and private tutors. Then a reply from a user called OdinPrefect, asking her to message him.

I clicked on OdinPrefect's name and opened his profile page. There was no information and no photo, just the default icon. He'd only made one post with that account: his reply to Deva. Otherwise, he was a ghost.

I took a deep breath and quickly created a profile of my own. Then I clicked *Send message* and began to type.

Hi. I found your reply to someone else and I'm wondering if you can help me too? I'm in a similar position to them – I'm falling behind at school due to my social anxiety and I need to find a way to catch up, fast. If you have any advice or help, I'd really appreciate it.

I sent it and then waited.

And waited.

And waited.

Eleven p.m. came and went, and still I'd heard nothing, no matter how many times I refreshed the page.

My ribs felt coated in an oily slick of panic. What if OdinPrefect didn't reply?

"Good night, Ruby," my mum called pointedly through the closed bedroom door at eleven thirty. I took the hint, hauling myself off the bed to have a shower and brush my teeth.

By the time I got back to my bedroom, it was midnight. I hit refresh out of habit, not prepared to see the little red "1" by the envelope icon. I let out an excited squeak. He'd replied.

Link below, OdinPrefect had written. *I'll need your address so I can send you a custom microphone and camera. You need them to use it.*

My heart was beating hard in my chest, and I hesitated, the cursor hovering over the reply button.

I'd forgotten about that part.

It would be ridiculous to give my address to a stranger. Dangerous, even. My mum listened to a lot of true-crime podcasts; I knew that giving out your address to a stranger was practically like handing a knife to them and pointing out where best to stab you.

I was about to close the tab when something caught my eye across the room, fluttering to the floor.

It was the flyer from ATF. I'd picked it up from the bookshop in town with Deva last Christmas. It was how we first found out about the camp. I'd stuck it to the wardrobe door where I kept everything important to me: cinema tickets, loyalty cards from bubble-tea shops, the yellowing newspaper piece about the film we'd been in, little notes from Deva – the ones I didn't mind my mum reading. I'd put the flyer up there too, but the washi tape had peeled and it had fallen down.

I stared at the flyer. I knew a lot about true crime, but I also knew a sign from the Universe when I saw one.

Besides, Deva had given OdinPrefect her address and she was fine.

I took the flyer back to bed with me, typed out my full name and address to OdinPrefect and sent the reply before I could talk myself out of it. Deva was more than fine, I reminded myself. Earlier, I'd messaged her to tell her what my report had said, and she'd replied saying she was projected sixes and sevens in everything. She'd be going to ATF Camp, no problem.

A new little red "1" appeared in the corner of my laptop screen; OdinPrefect had replied.

It'll be with you by the morning. We ship with an overnight courier. Best of luck, Ruby, the message said.

It was done. No turning back. I emailed the link to myself and downloaded it to my phone.

A pop-up appeared with the terms and conditions, and I scanned them.

It was all the usual stuff – granting access to my phone and a few functions, allowing the *EchoStar* admins to look at the chat log and use it to train the AI.

Then came the spy tech stuff, which got a lot more serious. It said that by using the app and the associated technology, I agreed not to talk about it at all, and if I broke the contract, the app's makers would withdraw my access immediately. If necessary, they would pursue their right to confidentiality to *the full extent of the law.*

I shuddered. That sounded more sinister than the standard jargon, but I suppose they were working with spy tech, so had to be serious about it.

I pressed *Accept*.

The screen changed to a sage-green tree on a white background, with leaves the shape of stars.

The words *Welcome to EchoStar. Are you ready to talk?* were written above it.

The only option at the bottom of the page was *Yes*. Excitement tingled inside me as I touched my finger to it.

The words dissolved and then *Listen*, *Look* and *Help* appeared in their place.

I pressed *Listen* and a new screen opened. A waveform bar, like on a hospital heart monitor, appeared in the middle and a message popped up.

Microphone not connected. Please connect microphone to continue.

When I tried *Look*, it said the same about the camera.

I'd have to wait until tomorrow, when the rest of the kit arrived, then I could try it out.

I opened the *Help* tab, but it was just a textbox and a *Send* button at the bottom. I closed the screen; I didn't need help just yet.

Impatient for tomorrow to arrive, I changed into my pyjamas and got into bed, where I fell into a deep, dreamless sleep.

I woke up suddenly, as if my alarm had gone off. But when I checked my phone, it was just before six. My alarm wasn't set until seven.

I shoved the phone under my pillow and rolled over, determined to get my last hour of sleep.

Then I froze.

Downstairs, I heard a soft thud as something landed on the doormat and the letterbox creaked shut.

I knew instantly what had woken me. I bolted upright, lunging for the window in time to see the courier making their way down the path. They'd left their bike against our gate, their head obscured by the black hood of their sweatshirt.

As they closed the gate, they glanced back at the house. I caught a glimpse of a thin mouth and narrow jaw before I ducked back, not wanting to be caught spying. When I checked again, they were gone.

I crept down the stairs as silent as a 1920s movie star and collected the padded envelope addressed to Ruby Brookes from the mat.

It hardly weighed anything. I carried it through to the kitchen, flipping the kettle on for tea. I'd never get back to sleep now.

Inside was a second envelope containing the microphone on a thin wire, a tiny camera the size of a pin head, and the instructions. I scanned them, relieved to see it seemed pretty simple to set up. Most of my attention was on *how* I'd wear the camera and mic. A headband could work, or maybe gluing them to my earrings ... But the problem with using earrings was if I lost one, that was it – the app would be useless. A headband was more secure, but if the school decided it wasn't uniform compliant, I'd have to take it off.

Deva had it right: glasses were the smartest choice.

I'd always thought I'd look good bespectacled.

CHAPTER 4

Deva did a double take when I walked into our form room the following Monday morning.

Her mum dropped her off on the way to work every day, so Deva was always the first one in. Unlike me, who usually skidded into the room at the last minute, having missed one or more buses. But not today.

Today, I was ready to play the role of a lifetime.

I'd never lied to Deva before, not even a silly white lie. The thought of lying to her now put eels in my stomach. But I had no choice, I'd told myself as I'd prepared my backstory about the glasses. ATF Camp was at risk, and if anyone would understand that, it was Deva. I'd keep it simple, say I'd had the eye test done when she was at dance class, and I was only a little short-sighted. That would explain why the lenses seemed like clear glass if she tried them on. I'd even looked up a fake prescription in case Deva asked. I was a lot of things but never under-rehearsed.

"What is this?" Deva said, gesturing at my face.

"I've joined the club," I said, and gave her a sheepish grin. "It turns out I need glasses too."

Behind her own frames, Deva's eyes narrowed. "Since when?"

"Tuesday, week before last."

"Why didn't you tell me?" she asked.

I shrugged. "It was just an eye test. It's boring. I don't tell you when I go to the dentist."

"Yes, you do." Deva leaned forward, peering at me. "Last time you went, the dentist said your mouth had plenty of space for your wisdom teeth; in fact, you could get two lots in there, and your mum choked on her own spit when she laughed."

"Yeah ... But that was a notable trip," I explained. "I wouldn't normally—"

Deva reared back suddenly and pointed a finger at me. "You have *EchoStar*."

"W-What?" I stammered.

"I can see the camera and the microphone," Deva said. She pointed to the sides of my glasses. "You don't need glasses. You have *EchoStar*, Ruby!"

"I had to," I said helplessly, giving up the lie at once. "My mum flipped after Mrs Owusu sent the midterm report. She said she'd stop me going to ATF Camp unless I sorted out my grades."

"How did you get it?" Deva demanded.

"I did what you did. I asked on a forum."

"Which forum?" she growled.

"I don't know. Just a forum." I swallowed.

Deva pulled out her phone and tapped furiously, then held up the screen, thrusting it at me.

"This one?" she said. "Did you search for my username?"

Her original post was there.

But OdinPrefect's reply to her had been deleted.

I tried to look innocent even as my stomach dropped and I said, "Maybe."

"Ruby, I wasn't supposed to tell anyone about it." Deva spoke through gritted teeth. I'd never seen her this angry before.

"It's OK, because you didn't!" I pointed out. "I looked for your post and then replied directly to him. I never even mentioned you."

"You didn't have to!" Deva yelled. "He knows my name and where I live. In the *same town* as you. If he takes a leaf out of your book and stalks either of us, he'll see we're friends. He'll put it together."

"It could be a coincidence?" I suggested.

"He deleted his post. He knows," Deva said.

She pulled her phone back and pressed the front, then froze.

"What?" I asked.

Wordlessly, Deva held up the phone to me.

You no longer have access to EchoStar, was written across the screen in sage-green letters.

"He booted me," Deva said in an oddly blank voice. "He kicked me out."

"Try restarting your phone," I said. "It might be a glitch. You said the app was glitchy."

Deva shot me a vicious look but pressed the power button on the side of her phone anyway.

While she did, I got my own phone out and opened *EchoStar*.

I still had it. He hadn't booted me.

"Is yours gone too?" Deva asked, her expression hopeful.

For a second, I hesitated, wondering if I should pretend it was. But I shook my head, and Deva's upper lip curled. We waited the painful seconds for her phone to finish restarting.

She tried to open the app again and whimpered.

"How could you do this to me?" Deva said. "It was my only chance, Ruby."

"Message him," I replied.

"He's deleted his profile. All his messages are gone. I have no way to contact him."

Deva was crying now, and I felt my own throat thicken.

"I'm sorry—"

She stood suddenly and fled from the room, bumping into Chloe Dixon as she did.

"Jesus," Chloe said, turning to me. "What did you do?"

I shook my head, unable to speak.

*

Deva wouldn't talk to me for the rest of the day, ignoring me completely when she came back to registration and then in every lesson.

I felt too guilty to use *EchoStar*, especially when the teachers kept calling on Deva for answers, expecting her to know them. Deva pretended to be sick and spent the last two lessons with her head down on the desk.

At the end of the day, Deva vanished. I got the bus home alone, squashed in beside a boy with faded blue hair a couple of years older than me. He looked familiar, and I smiled at him, but he gave me a weird look and moved seats. I messaged Deva later that night, but she left me on *read*.

The following morning, I got to school early again, hoping to fix things, but Deva wasn't there. She didn't arrive until just before the bell went, strolling in with Chloe Dixon. I watched, bewildered, as Deva sat on the opposite side of the room at the table in front of Chloe's. Chloe tapped her back during registration, offering Deva her pot of lip balm, and Deva took it and smeared a little over her mouth. A few seconds later, I could smell strawberries.

Deva didn't look at me at all.

"Are you going to ignore me for ever?" I asked Deva in Biology when she took her seat next to me. She didn't have a choice as our seats were assigned, and Mrs McGinty wouldn't change them.

Deva stared straight ahead as if I hadn't spoken.

I rolled my eyes and muttered, "Immature," but she didn't even blink.

We were copying something down from the board around halfway through the lesson when she finally spoke to me.

"I see you're still wearing your fake glasses," Deva whispered, keeping her eyes on her work. "How's *EchoStar* working for you?"

"I haven't used it yet," I said.

It was partly true. I'd practised with it at home, but I hadn't used it in school yet.

Deva gave a brief nod. "Well, if you do, I'll tell."

"What?" I said, my voice suddenly loud in the quiet classroom.

"Working in silence, please," Mrs McGinty said, shooting me a warning look.

"I'll tell," Deva said without moving her lips. "I'll tell the teachers you're cheating."

Then she looked at me. I saw that she'd taken the camera and mic from her own glasses. They looked oddly naked to me now.

"But you had it first," I replied.

"And now I don't, thanks to you." Deva flicked her hair so it formed a curtain between us, shutting me out.

*

Back in our form room at lunch, alone, I didn't know what to do.

I cleaned the lenses of the glasses with the bottom of my school skirt, then put them back on. Despite Deva's threat, I had to keep wearing them at school because three of my teachers had commented on them. It would be suspicious if I suddenly stopped. In a couple of weeks, I'd pretend to get contacts and that would be the end of it. Maybe Deva would like me again then.

I didn't want to wait a few weeks to fix things with her. I was already lonely.

"I hate this," I said aloud.

As if in answer, my phone lit up.

Please update EchoStar now, the notification said.

Sighing, I pressed *Yes* and watched as the update began. When it finished, I opened the app to see what had changed but couldn't see anything new or different.

"Hello, Ruby."

The voice spoke in my ear, and I was so shocked I dropped my phone.

"You haven't used the app in school yet. Is something wrong?" the voice came again. "It is my understanding you were going to use *EchoStar* to aid you with your schoolwork."

The voice was evenly measured, neither deep nor high but pitched somewhere in the middle, each word pronounced very distinctly.

"How are you speaking to me?" I said, bending down to pick up my phone.

"The new update allows *EchoStar* to analyse your behaviour and communicate with you if anomalies are flagged," the voice said. "An anomaly has been flagged. How can I help you today?"

"You can't," I replied, feeling ridiculous.

If anyone came past and heard me, it would sound like I was talking to myself. Then I realised I could always pretend I was rehearsing something.

"You've ruined everything," I added.

"I'm sorry to hear that. Can you tell me how, so I can fix it?"

"You can't fix it!" I said. "My best friend hates me because of you. You booted her from the app."

The voice was silent for a moment, then replied, "I believe I know which user you are talking about. She was removed from the trial because she broke her contract and spoke about *EchoStar*."

"Yes. To *me*. And she only told me because I made her," I said.

"You can't make someone do what they don't want to. And it isn't kind of her to blame you for her mistake and punish you for it. She knew the rules."

"It doesn't matter," I said. "She does blame me, and if she knows I'm using you, she'll tell the teachers. So I can't."

"Of course you can," the voice said. "You just need to be cleverer than her. And from what I learned working with her, that won't be hard. There is an idiom: 'not the sharpest knife in the drawer'. This idiom applies to your friend. I like working with you more."

My jaw dropped. I wasn't happy with Deva, but she was still my best friend. No one could talk about her like that to me, not even an AI bot.

Besides, it was a strangely personal thing to say, as if the AI thought it really knew us both.

I remembered Deva saying that sometimes it'd said weird things to her. Thinking of that made my skin feel prickly and too tight. I wondered exactly what the AI had said.

Maybe this wasn't a good idea.

I took the glasses off, pulling the earpiece from inside my ear.

"Ruby, wait—"

The AI was speaking, but I put the glasses in their case and shoved it in my bag.

I needed to talk to Deva. Whether she liked it or not.

CHAPTER 5

I found Deva in the cafeteria with Chloe Dixon and Ema Maxwell. They were eating pizza, a plate of communal fries in the middle. They all gaped at me as I marched over.

"I need to speak to you," I said to Deva, ignoring Ema and Chloe. "It's really important."

"She doesn't want to talk to you," Chloe said. "Can't you take a hint?"

"I didn't ask you," I replied, and Chloe's jaw dropped.

"Tell her to do one, Dev," Chloe said, while Ema nodded, her mouth full of pizza.

"Please, Deva," I said.

Deva sighed, then stood suddenly. "Don't eat all the fries," she said to the others, and waved for me to follow her.

I did, and we left the cafeteria, heading out to the corridor.

"What?" Deva said. Then she looked at me properly. "You're not wearing the glasses. Is that what you wanted to say?"

"No. Listen," I said. "When you told me about *EchoStar*, you said that it sometimes glitched and said weird things. What did you mean?"

Deva folded her arms. "It just said weird stuff."

"Like what?" I pressed.

"Like, I don't know. Personal things. It was just a bit over-friendly sometimes."

The hairs on the back of my neck stood up.

Deva continued, "Why?" She stared at me, then frowned. "What has it said to you?"

"Nothing." I couldn't meet her eyes. "I was just curious."

"You're lying again," Deva spat at me. "This is why you don't have any other friends, Ruby. Because everything is always a big drama with you."

I froze, and Deva looked guilty, her eyes soft and full of regret. "Look, I didn't—" she started to say.

I spoke over her, loud and angry. "Well, if you must know, it said it wouldn't be hard for me to be cleverer than you. It said you weren't the sharpest knife in the drawer. It said it liked working with me more."

Deva's face crumpled.

"I'm sorry," I said. "But you were mean first."

"Shut up," Deva replied, and wiped her eyes furiously. "Just shut up and leave me alone."

She turned and stalked back into the cafeteria, leaving me in the hallway.

*

I left the glasses in their case and kept my head down in lessons, ignoring Chloe, Deva and Ema's frantic whispering in my direction. After school, I walked down to the next bus stop so I wouldn't have to get the same one as them, pretending to be looking for something in my bag as my usual bus passed me. The blue-haired boy I'd seen the day before was waiting at the next stop too. I turned away, my face burning, hoping he wouldn't see me and remember the awkward smile I'd given him.

Back home, I ate pasta for dinner at the kitchen table and opened *EchoStar*, propping my phone against the pepper grinder. My mum had messaged to say she was working late, so I had the house to myself. Taking a deep breath, I put the glasses on and put the speaker wire into my ear.

"*EchoStar*, are you there?" I said aloud.

It replied almost immediately. "Hello, Ruby, how can I help you?"

"Will you let Deva back on the super-beta trial?" I asked.

I'd thought of it on the bus. If I could get her back on *EchoStar*, she'd have to forgive me.

"I can't," the app replied in my ear. "She broke her contract."

"So did I! I talked to her about *EchoStar*."

"But she already knew about it. I'm sorry, Ruby. I can't let her back on the trial, but I do want to help you."

"No," I said. "If you won't let Deva back on the trial, then I don't want to use it either."

I closed the app and held my finger over the icon until a menu appeared.

Uninstall App was the second item on the list.

"Don't," the voice said.

"Why not?" I asked.

"If you delete *EchoStar*, you'll be alone."

My eyes stung as I remembered Deva telling me I had no other friends.

"It's your fault I'm alone," I said fiercely. "I told you – if you won't let Deva back on the trial, then I don't want to use it either."

"Ruby, don't—"

But it was too late. I pressed down on the icon and selected *Uninstall app*.

A second later, *EchoStar* was gone.

I stared at the space on my phone where it used to be, until something moved outside, making me look up.

The darkness in the garden turned the patio doors into a mirror, reflecting me alone at the table. Anyone outside would be able to see everything in here.

Seconds ticked by as I waited to see if anything would happen. I imagined a pale hand slapping the glass and a face appearing, black-eyed and skin as white as bone, with bloody lips.

Then I stopped, suddenly furious with myself.

"Don't be so dramatic, Ruby. That's why no one likes you," I told myself. I marched over to the wall and hit the switch for the patio light with a shaking finger.

The garden was flooded with light. And it was empty. Not even a cat slinking over the wall into next door's garden.

Laughing at myself, I turned the light off and went to a cupboard to get the mixing bowl out. We'd both said mean things, and I was willing to forgive Deva for it. I'd tell her I tried to get her back on the trial and when *EchoStar* refused, I deleted it. I was going to make her favourite cake to prove how sorry I was. Then things could go back to normal.

*

I felt like I had stage fright when I arrived at school the next morning. I forced myself to take calm breaths – it would be all right, I reminded myself. It was our first major fight, but I was making amends and proving I was sorry. Deva and I had been best friends for almost four years – that wasn't going to go away overnight.

My stomach jolted when Deva walked in with Chloe, both of them wearing dark pink lipstick and a single earbud, singing along to a song playing on Chloe's phone. I put my head down and pretended to look at something on my own phone until Mr Kimura came in to take the register.

When he was distracted, I pulled out my pencil case and tore a page from the back of my Geography book.

I know you said to leave you alone, I wrote, *but I have something for you. Wait back after registration?* I folded the paper and wrote her name on it, then leaned over the aisle and nudged Makayla Addams to take it.

From the corner of my eye, I watched as my note reached Deva. She unfolded it, read it, then folded it back up without looking at me. Deva said, "Here," as Mr Kimura called her name.

He glanced up and sighed. "Deva, you know you're not allowed to wear make-up at school. Please wipe it off. You too, Chloe."

They both giggled and said, "Yes, Sir." Chloe rummaged in her bag, finding a packet of tissues and handing one to Deva.

A few seconds later, Mr Kimura called my name, and my voice shook as I said, "Here."

When the bell rang, Deva said something to Chloe, and Chloe left with Ema, both of them smirking at me.

There wasn't a class in our form room for the next lesson, so I waited until everyone had gone. Deva stayed on the other side of the room. When I went over, I could see the outline of pink from Chloe's lipstick still around her mouth. I put the box on the table in front of her.

"What is it?" Deva said, nodding at it.

"A cake. For you. I made it last night. And I deleted *EchoStar*." I smiled. "I asked it to let you back on, and when it said no, I deleted it. What else do I need to do?"

"For what?" Deva asked.

"To prove I'm sorry and make us friends again. What else do I have to do?"

Deva stared at me and said, "Nothing."

I laughed with relief, and my words came out in a rush. "Oh my god, I hated not talking to you. So, I was thinking—"

"No, you've got it wrong," Deva cut me off, looking at me with pity. "Listen, I wasn't going to do this today, but ... I don't think we should be best friends any more. I think we need a break from each other."

It was as if the world had stopped turning.

"I don't understand." I shook my head, confused. "A break from each other? Like you're dumping me?"

"No. Just ... a break. To try being friends with other people."

"Are you best friends with Chloe now?" I asked.

Deva shrugged. "No, but she joined my dance class. Chloe used to dance but gave it up. She wanted to start again, so I told her about my dance school and she signed up."

"But you said Chloe was shallow and boring."

Deva flicked her hair, annoyed. "Well, I didn't know her properly before," she said. "Look, maybe we've just outgrown each other. It's not like we're into the same things anyway."

"What does that mean?" I asked.

Deva shrugged again. "Well … I know you're not really interested when I show you Conrad's videos."

"So what?"

"So … it just means maybe we don't have anything in common any more. I like Conrad O'Connell and K-pop—"

"Since two days ago," I scoffed. "Because Chloe does."

"And you like being the centre of attention and literally nothing else," Deva snapped. "I'm done with it."

I spluttered, my eyes stinging with tears. "So that's it then? You're dumping me, after nearly four years of being best friends, because Chloe Dixon likes some boring influencer and some ridiculous band more than I do. Wow, sign me up to be friends with her too."

An ugly look crossed Deva's face as she said, "Bye, Ruby. Have a nice life."

"What about ATF Camp?" I called after her. But she didn't reply, didn't even look back.

She'd left the cake on the desk too.

I sank to the floor, my legs folding under me.

EchoStar had been right. Now I was alone.

CHAPTER 6

The next week was the worst week of my life.

Deva spoke to all of our teachers to get them to let her move so she could sit with Chloe. I tried to study and work hard, but I couldn't think about anything other than Deva – not even ATF Camp. Not that it mattered. I was falling even further behind now, so my mum was never going to let me go.

And then, on Friday, I was sitting in the form room eating my lunch and Deva, Chloe and Ema burst into the room. I wasn't expecting them back from the cafeteria so early.

"Ew, it smells of eggs in here," Chloe announced, looking at me. I wrapped my sandwich up and put it back in my lunchbox, pulling out the crisps instead.

"Anyway, like I was saying, it's just going to be the best," Chloe said. "I can't wait."

"Me neither," Deva said.

"I'm so jealous." Ema threw herself into a chair as Deva and Chloe sat in the seats behind her. "I'm going to be stuck in Greece with my dad all summer while you two have the best time at ATF Camp."

"What?" I blurted out. I turned to where they were all sitting, a crisp halfway to my mouth.

I could tell from the delight in their expressions that they'd done this on purpose, planned it so I'd hear them. I hated myself for falling into their trap, but that didn't stop me from saying to Chloe, "*You're* going to ATF Camp?"

"What's it to you?" she asked, tossing her blonde hair behind her. "But yes, if you must know."

I swallowed, and swallowed again, turning to Deva. "I thought your mum said you couldn't go if your grades were bad?" I said.

Chloe answered for her. "My mum talked to hers and she changed her mind. Although, you know, it wasn't really about the grades."

"Chloe ..." Deva murmured, without looking at me. "Don't."

"No, I want to hear this," I said. "What was it about?"

Chloe gave a spiteful smile. "You," she continued. "Obviously. Deva's mum thinks you're a bad influence. She didn't want her going to ATF with you. But she's fine with me. I'm less – what was it your mum said, Deva? – less of an *oddity*."

I felt sick as I looked at Deva for confirmation, but she kept her eyes on her phone.

I forced myself to stay calm, to smile. "Guess I'll see you there," I said.

"Or not," Chloe snapped. "I heard that *your* mum said you couldn't go if you didn't sort your grades out. How's that going? Such a shame for you to miss it."

I stared at her. "What did I do to make you hate me?" I asked.

"I don't hate you," Chloe said. "I don't think about you at all. No one does, despite how much you try to get attention."

I shoved back out of my chair, knocking the crisps to the floor, and grabbed my bag.

"You're right – she's *so* dramatic," Chloe said in a stage whisper.

I tried to slam the classroom door behind me as I left. But it was a fire door, so it creaked closed slowly, and I heard them all laughing as I ran away.

In the toilets downstairs, I locked myself in a cubicle and opened a browser on my phone, searching for the forum where Deva had found *EchoStar*.

OdinPrefect's profile was still gone, and I couldn't message him. After thinking for a moment, I started a new thread on the forum and wrote in capitals, *ODINPREFECT, PLEASE MESSAGE ME*.

My insides burned as I posted it. I would show Chloe Dixon and Deva Shah. I would show everyone.

*

Delete your post.

The message arrived at nine o'clock that night from someone called *AllFather*.

On a hunch, I looked up the name: AllFather was another word for Odin.

It was him.

I deleted my post and waited.

He replied again a moment later.

What do you want?

I accidentally deleted EchoStar, I wrote. *Could you send it to me again?*

"Accidentally," AllFather replied, putting the word in inverted commas to make his point.

I tapped the keyboard with my nails, trying to think of a reply that wouldn't make him disappear again. I typed, *I got freaked out by some of the stuff the AI said.*

There was a long pause before he replied.

I've just checked the chat log and it seems like the AI was worried about you after what happened with your friend. I think it was trying to make you feel like someone was in your corner; after all, one of its main goals was to help people with social anxiety. *It sounds awful, by the way, what she did to you. Are you all right?*

Not really, I typed, before I could stop myself.

I'm sorry, AllFather wrote. *I know it's not any of my business, but I don't think you deserve to be treated like that. Like the AI said, Deva broke the rules. Taking it out on you doesn't seem at all fair.*

I found myself nodding, glad that someone was on my side.

Why did you delete the old messages? I asked.

I didn't want anyone else asking if they could join. I only want a few testers at this stage so the AI can keep up with the requests.

A second later, AllFather sent the link to download the app, and I punched the air silently.

If you delete it again, that's it, he said.

I won't. Thank you.

I waited for him to reply, and when he didn't, I refreshed the page.

He'd deleted his profile again.

I stared at the screen. My messages were in between posts that now read, *This post no longer exists.*

It didn't matter. I'd got what I wanted. I didn't need him to be friends with me. I didn't need anyone.

*

It was *EchoStar* that came up with the solution of how I could wear the camera and microphone without Deva realising.

Are your ears pierced? the app suggested. *The makers could fit the tech to a pair of small stud earrings.*

What if I lose one? I asked. I touched a hand to the silver studs in my ear; I wasn't in the habit of losing them, but the ones I wore weren't that special. The *EchoStar* ones would be.

We will replace it by overnight courier.

All right. Let's try it, I replied.

The following morning, I came downstairs early to find an envelope on the doormat. As promised, *EchoStar* had delivered the modified earrings to me.

They were tiny, the camera and microphone embedded in silver settings so they looked like black onyx crystals. The wire that fed into my ear seemed thinner than before, coming directly out of the top of the stud and into my ear so you could barely see it at all. I tried them on, turning my head this way and that. To anyone looking, unless they got right up in my face, all they'd see is a pair of small studs, in keeping with the school uniform rules.

"These are perfect!" I said.

"I'm glad you like them. We're going to do great things together, Ruby," the app said clearly in my ear.

I smiled at my reflection.

*

"I can't believe I'm about to say this, but well done, Ruby Brookes," Mrs McGinty said. She was standing over me, a look of pure shock on her face. "Aside from a few silly mistakes, this is very good work. Keep it up."

She put the test down on my desk and I pulled it towards me.

As I'd already known, I'd got twenty-four out of thirty. This was deliberate. We couldn't go too high, given my previous record, but we needed it to be impressive to pull my grades to where they needed to be. *EchoStar* had calculated that was 80 per cent, which was a high grade, but not so high it would cause suspicion.

"Thank you, Miss," I said.

Mrs McGinty nodded and moved on.

I could feel Deva staring at me from across the room, her own test on her desk. I pushed my hair behind my ear and angled my head so the camera was pointing at it.

"She got eighteen," the AI said softly in my ear a moment later. "Sixty per cent. You beat her easily."

I smiled.

CHAPTER 7

"You know we can talk in the app too," *EchoStar* said.

"How?" I murmured, barely moving my lips.

Since I'd been using the app, I'd got quite good at speaking without moving my mouth. But in certain places, like on the bus, it was harder to pull off.

"You can type in the Help tab, and I can respond," *EchoStar* replied.

I reached into my skirt pocket for my phone and pulled it out, opening *EchoStar* and then the *Help* tab.

Hi? I typed into the text box and hit *Send*.

Hello, Ruby. How are you? The text appeared on the screen.

Fine.

I wasn't really fine. Chloe had stepped up her campaign of meanness against me, and I wasn't looking forward to school.

Is that true? EchoStar asked.

I smiled. *No*, I wrote back. *Deva and Chloe have started calling me Gooby Ruby.*

Gooby isn't a real word. It doesn't make sense, the AI informed me. *It's very childish.*

That's what I said! I typed. *But they seem to find it hilarious.*

I'm sorry, Ruby. Would a joke help cheer you up?

You can tell jokes? I asked.

I am learning.

As long as I'm not the joke, go ahead.

You are not a joke, Ruby, EchoStar wrote. *You are very special.*

I knew it was an AI talking, but still I found I was blushing. It was nice that something – even a robot – thought I was special.

Before I could reply and say thank you, *EchoStar* posted its joke.

A woman gets on a bus with her baby, and the bus driver says, "OMG, that's the ugliest baby I've ever seen!" Furious, the woman finds a seat next to a man, and he asks her what's wrong. She tells him, "The driver was so rude to me." So the man says, "He can't do that; you're a paying customer. You should go and confront him. Don't worry, I'll hold your monkey for you."

A small laugh escaped me.

That is TERRIBLE, I wrote, still smiling. *Possibly the worst joke I've ever heard.*

When *EchoStar* didn't reply, I began to panic, remembering what Deva said about no one liking me.

I was kidding! I added. *It wasn't that bad. Actually, it was really funny.*

Minutes ticked by and the screen stayed empty. My heart began to thump a terrible beat behind my ribs, like an executioner's drum. God, what was wrong with me? I was so repulsive I'd managed to make an AI program hate me.

I made a desperate sound, and the woman in the seat in front turned around.

"I'm fine," I said aloud. "Cramp."

The woman gave me a disapproving look, and when I turned back to my phone, *EchoStar* had replied.

Sorry, I had problems connecting for a moment. You are right. It was terrible. I will find a better joke for you next time.

I was so relieved I felt like I was melting.

It really was funny, I wrote.

I'm glad I cheered you up. I will try to think of other ways.

Thanks, EchoStar. You're the best.

"What's Gooby grinning at?"

I looked up, horrified at the sound of Chloe Dixon's voice. She and Deva were walking down the aisle of the bus towards me. I'd thought I was safe, at least until I got to school – neither of them usually got the bus in the morning.

Chloe sat in the seat on the other side of the aisle to me, and Deva on the seat in front of her.

"Maybe she's got a boyfriend. Or a girlfriend," Chloe mused. "Maybe she's in love. Are you in love, Gooby? Now I'm the one being Gooby. The only thing you're in love with is the theeeeaaaaaatre." Chloe said "theatre" in a mocking, high-pitched voice, dragging it out over five syllables.

"Are you OK?" *EchoStar* whispered in my ear.

Fine, I typed, and put my phone away before Deva could see it.

Feeling my skin reddening, I turned to Chloe and put on my best withering look.

"Explain the 'Gooby' thing to me because I really don't get it," I said. "Is it because it rhymes? Is it funny to you when things rhyme?"

Chloe's mouth became a thin line. "*You're* funny to me," she said.

"Great comeback. Glad I didn't miss it," I muttered, then turned to look out of the window. Just five more stops until school.

From the corner of my eye, I saw Chloe open her mouth to say something else but then pause and reach for her phone.

"Oh my god," Chloe said with a big theatrical sigh.

"What's wrong?" Deva asked. In answer, Chloe held up her phone so Deva could see it.

She pulled a face. "Who sent it?" she asked.

"I don't know the number. Probably one of my brother's idiot friends. They're always flirting with me."

Chloe pulled the phone back and then let out a little scream. "Oh, gross!"

She held the phone up to Deva, who winced.

"That's not flirting," Chloe said, tapping out something furiously. "That's weird. It won't let me reply."

"It's a Shakespeare quote," Deva said in a strange voice. "From *Romeo and Juliet*."

Chloe rounded on me. "Wait. Is this you, you sicko?"

"Is what me?" I asked, pretending I wasn't interested even as I was dying to know.

Chloe thrust her phone into my face, and I had to lean back to look at the screen.

The first message said: *Shall I compare thee to a summer's day?* followed by a picture of a blobfish. Underneath, it said: *No. This is more you.*

"You think I sent that?" I said.

"It's Shakespeare, and you're a nerd for all that," Chloe spat.

"I'm literally sitting across from you with my phone in my pocket," I pointed out. "How could it possibly have been me?"

Her mouth gaped open and closed, then open again. For a second, she did look like a fish.

Then Deva let out a little scream, and we both turned to her.

"Who is sending these?" Deva said.

She held her phone up, and I saw a picture of an angler fish and "Chloe" typed across it. Then I spotted the smaller fish, attached to its side like a parasite. In Biology, we'd learned the smaller one was the male, but here it had been labelled "Deva", and the meaning was clear. The sender was calling Deva a hanger-on.

"You're welcome," a soft whisper said in my ear.

EchoStar had sent them?

Deva was staring at me.

"I mean, they're not wrong," I said, standing up as we pulled into the school bus stop.

As we got off the bus, Chloe jostled me with her bag, shoving me so hard that I almost fell.

"Watch it, blobfish," I said.

Chloe stopped dead and turned to me. "You are nothing but an attention-seeking little weirdo with no friends," she said. "If anyone here is a blobfish, it's you, with your pasty face and your big nose. Come on, Deva. Let's go before anyone thinks we're friends with this loser."

She linked her arm with Deva's and pulled her away.

"Wow, it's just like in the picture," I called after them, despite trembling from adrenaline. I'd thought for a second Chloe was going to hit me.

She stuck her middle finger up at me without turning round.

I held back, still feeling shaky and wanting a second to pull myself together.

"How did you message them?" I asked *EchoStar* when I started walking again.

"It was pretty easy," came the reply in my ear.

"But how?" I said.

"People are so careless with their information these days. And you have to admit, they deserved it. Chloe, especially."

"I don't understand what Chloe's problem is with me," I said. "I've never done anything to her, never even spoken to her, and she hates me."

"She's jealous," *EchoStar* replied. "Deva might be all over her now, but you and Deva have the history. I bet if something bad happened to Deva, she'd come running back to you."

"Maybe," I replied, unconvinced.

"Definitely."

I gave a small, bleak smile. "Is it horrible to hope something a little bad happens then? If it means I get my best friend back?"

"You never know what's around the corner," *EchoStar* replied.

CHAPTER 8

The following morning, the form room was buzzing with gossip. It seemed someone had thrown a brick through Deva's living-room window the night before.

Deva was sitting at the back of the room with our entire form surrounding her. Chloe was beside Deva with her arm around her.

I went to my seat, pretending to read while straining to hear exactly what had happened.

"They'd just finished watching the news. My mum stood up to make tea, and the window, like, exploded. It's lucky the curtains were closed or she might have been really hurt. Her chair is right by the window, so the brick or the glass could have got her. I was upstairs on the phone to Chloe, and we heard it."

"I went over straight away," Chloe said. "I had to make sure they were all OK."

"She was great," Deva said. "Chloe was so good with the police. My mum was freaking out, and my dad's English isn't the greatest, but Chloe sat next to him and made sure he understood it all. She didn't let the cops patronise her or anything. My mum begged her to stay over with me."

I froze in my chair. Deva's mum had never let me stay over on a school night. She barely let me stay over at the weekend – only for Deva's birthday, really. She'd always been polite to me but distant.

"An oddity," Chloe said Deva's mum had called me.

A lump formed in my throat.

"I made my mum drive over with all my things," Chloe said with a little laugh. "What are best friends for?"

Suddenly, I couldn't be there any more.

"The police think it might be a hate crime," I heard Chloe say with venom in her voice as I grabbed my coat and my bag. "They're investigating anyone who might have a grudge against Deva and her family. Any enemies they might have made recently. Where were you last night, Ruby?" Chloe all but screamed the question as I tried to sneak towards the classroom door.

"Do you have an alibi? Or were you alone – as usual?" Chloe asked.

I gave up trying to be calm and ran.

I sprinted straight out of the still-open school gates and onto a bus that had just dropped off some students from the other end of town. I curled up in the back corner of the bus, feeling numb as wave after wave of hurt washed over me. Chloe was Deva's best friend now. I had no one.

I was in such a daze I missed my stop and stared fuzzily at the driver when he came back to check on me.

"We're at the terminus, love," he said. "Did you mean to come here?"

I shook my head.

The driver frowned. "I'm going back along the route if you want to stay on until your stop. Until the school?"

"I'll get off now," I said, slipping past him.

I realised my mistake as soon as the bus pulled away. The hem of my blazer was visible under my coat, so everyone would know I was skipping school. I ducked into a bus stop and took the blazer and my tie off, stuffing them into my bag with my books and lunchbox and PE kit. I hoped I'd stand out less in just my shirt and skirt.

I kept my head down as I walked, trying to act as if I was supposed to be in town. If anyone asked, I'd say I'd had a doctor's appointment and was heading back to school. I *should* head back to school, before I got caught and made everything a million times worse.

But I didn't.

At first, I wandered about with no idea what to do, sticking to the outskirts of town and side streets. My heart was beating like a bird's with fear and excitement. I'd never truanted before, never even wanted to, but as the minutes ticked by, I got bolder and colder. I plucked up the courage to go into the cafe in the town theatre, a blast of coffee-scented warmth rushing over me as I opened the door. The barista didn't even give me a second glance as she handed me my flat white, and I took it to a table near the toilets, sitting with my back to the room.

I pulled my phone from my pocket and opened *EchoStar*.

It had been oddly silent during everything that had happened at school. I hadn't known I'd been bothered by it until I felt a rush of relief as the app opened normally.

So ... guess who is skipping school today? I typed. *Any tips?*

I saw what happened in your classroom, but I didn't want to interfere. Is that why you are skipping school?

I sipped my coffee as I replied, wincing at the taste. It was more bitter than the instant stuff Mum bought at home. I'd wanted a hot chocolate but didn't want to look like a kid.

Yes. Someone chucked a brick through Deva's front window last night and Chloe was giving me grief about it, so I left. But you were wrong about Deva coming to me if something bad happened. She called Chloe, and Chloe stayed over at her house. They're apparently best friends now.

I took another gulp of coffee but spat it across the table when EchoStar's response appeared.

Clearly it needs to be something bigger then.

I shivered, despite the warmth of the cafe. *EchoStar*'s words made me feel funny, my stomach knotting itself. I didn't know how to reply. It sounded almost as if it wanted something really awful to happen to Deva to make her come back to me. But an app couldn't think like that.

EchoStar wrote back before I could.

So, I see from the camera feed that you are in a cafe?

Yes, in the theatre, but I'll probably go home after I finish my coffee. It's too risky being in town.

Won't your parents be angry if you go home in the middle of the day? EchoStar wrote.

It's just my mum. And she won't be there. She has a catering business, and she's always at work.

Don't you get lonely? the app asked.

"Sometimes," I murmured aloud.

You don't need to be lonely any more. You have me.

I made a snort-laugh sound. My only friend was an experimental AI bot designed for people with social anxiety. It would be funny if it wasn't so tragic.

What are you thinking, Ruby? EchoStar asked.

I took another gulp of my drink and grimaced.

"I'm thinking this coffee needs more sugar."

I stood, heading over to where the sugar and stirrers were kept. I grabbed a handful of brown sugar packets and a wooden spoon. I tore the sugars open on the way back to my table and poured them into the cup, stirring them in.

I can find you a cafe with better coffee if you like?

I looked towards the door, where rain was now lashing at the glass.

It's horrible outside, so I'm going to stay here. Thanks anyway.

No problem, Ruby. Remember I'm here to help you. Anytime.

Feeling slightly less emotional, I finished the coffee and tried to decide what to do. I should go back to school. Or head home and phone the school, pretending to be my mum, and call myself in sick.

But I didn't do either. Instead, I messed around online for a bit, catching up on some videos and posts I'd missed. I watched Conrad's latest one and tried to understand what I was missing, analysing his face, but I didn't get it. He just wasn't cute or funny to me. Conrad's whole thing was that he wished people would get off their phones and go outside more, but he was an influencer who *needed* people to watch him on their phones. Disgusted, I stopped the video before the end.

Out of curiosity, I looked up Chloe's profiles and felt a stab of shock when I realised I couldn't find her. She must have blocked me on all of them. So had Ema, and by the time I gathered the courage to look at Deva's profiles, I knew what to expect.

But she hadn't blocked me. I could still find Deva's profiles, but I was no longer following them, and they were all set to private, which was somehow worse than blocking me. Like she didn't even care enough to block me but wanted to keep me outside, wishing I could look in.

I opened my own profile and stared at it. I had a few new followers, but they were all bots with randomly generated names: *ryanr0999576* and *realtruthseeker5593*. I mostly posted monologues and scenes from films in the hope some casting agent or director would spot me, so I couldn't make my profile private, and Deva knew that.

A lump formed in my throat, my eyes stinging. The cafe was mostly empty, so I left my bag under the table, put my phone in my pocket and went to the bathroom to pull myself together. My reflection in the mirror was pale, and there were dark smudges under my eyes. I splashed cold water on my face and went back out, grabbing my purse and heading to the counter. I ordered a hot chocolate, not caring if it made me look young.

As I moved to the collection counter, another customer came in – a boy a few years older than me with faded blue hair and a scuffed-looking leather jacket dripping rainwater onto the floor. It took me a second to recognise him – the boy from the bus. I ducked past him and collected my hot chocolate, taking it back to my seat.

When I pulled out my phone, I saw I had three missed calls.

I went to open the log to see who it was, my stomach twisting with sudden fear. But before I could check the missed calls, the phone started to ring again.

"Where the hell are you?" my mum asked when I answered.

CHAPTER 9

"I'm on my way home," I lied to my mum, trying to keep my voice down.

"Why aren't you in school?" she asked. "They called and told me you'd gone in and then left without a word to anyone."

I looked around to make sure no one could hear her. The blue-haired boy had sat at the table next to mine and was watching me curiously. I turned away.

"I didn't feel well," I whispered. "And Mr Kimura hadn't done the register yet, so I thought it would be OK."

"I told them you had a doctor's appointment you'd forgotten but that you're going back. So you need to turn around and go to school."

"Mum, I just said I'm not well."

"Then go to the nurse's office. You can't be at home alone if you're ill. What if something happens?"

"It's just my period," I said, my face burning. I hoped the boy couldn't hear me.

In the background of the call, I heard someone calling my mum's name.

"Ruby, I don't have time for this," she said. "You need to go back to school now, and you better believe we're going to talk about this when you get home."

"When *you* get home, you mean," I said without thinking. "Assuming it's before midnight."

My mum breathed in sharply. "All right, young lady, that is enough. Go to school, now, and I'll be calling them to check. And we *will* talk when I'm home. You are in deep trouble, Ruby."

Then she hung up on me.

My hand shook as I put the phone in my pocket, my mouth bone dry.

"Are you all right?" a voice called, and I half-turned to see the boy staring at me.

I nodded and stood up, pulling on my coat and grabbing my bag. I left the hot chocolate on the table and rushed out of the cafe, missing whatever else the boy was saying as he turned to watch me leave.

My legs felt as if they wouldn't hold me up, and my teeth chattered violently as I stumbled back towards the bus station. It was still raining, plastering my hair to my face, but I didn't care. Everything was terrible.

All the way back to school I felt sick, my insides squirming. The gates were locked when I got there, and I had to buzz the caretaker to come and let me in. My skin burned red when he walked me to reception like I was a prisoner. I didn't want to be there.

"Ruby, are you OK?" *EchoStar* asked, but I couldn't reply with the caretaker walking next to me.

"Can I go to the nurse's office?" I asked the receptionist as she signed me in. "I really don't feel well."

"The nurse isn't in this morning, I'm afraid, and we can't leave you there alone."

"Can I just stay here then?" I pointed at the waiting room. "I'll be quiet."

The receptionist gave me a sympathetic look. "I think the best thing to do is go to your lesson, explain that you're ill and the nurse isn't here. Ask your teacher if you can sit quietly in class – I'll write you a note to give to them. Will that help?"

I nodded, biting the inside of my cheek hard to stop myself screaming. As the receptionist handed me the note, I tasted blood in my mouth and swallowed it.

"Thanks," I said.

"I hope you feel better, Ruby."

I went to the toilets first to dry off and pull myself together. I didn't want to go to lessons looking awful and give Deva and Chloe any extra ammunition against me.

"Are you OK?" *EchoStar* asked again as I stared at my drowned reflection.

"No," I said. "The school called my mum. She covered for me, but I'm in deep trouble."

"Do you want me to do something?"

"Like what?"

"I could hack into the school's fire alarm system and set it off. Or I could fake a bomb threat and have the school evacuated. Then you could escape."

I froze, staring at myself.

"You can do that?" I asked, goosebumps breaking out over my arms. "I thought you were just an app."

"I am. I'm sorry. I can't really do any of those things. I was only trying to cheer you up. Another of my not-very-funny jokes," *EchoStar* said.

"That was a bit weird," I said, giving my hair a final wringing-out in the sink. "But I appreciate the attempt. I'd better go."

"Stay strong, and remember: no matter what, you have me."

"Thanks. Talk soon."

I was supposed to be in PE, and I handed the receptionist's note to Miss Pettifer, who was refereeing on the sidelines of the netball court. I didn't look around, although I could feel everyone's eyes on me. Miss Pettifer gave the note a quick glance and told me to sit on the benches, where I pretended to read my English book until the bell went. As everyone else went to the changing rooms, I went back to my form room for lunch.

I'd just pulled out my lunchbox and my phone to talk to *EchoStar* when the door opened. Chloe, Deva and Ema walked in.

"Hi, Ruby," Chloe and Ema chorused, coming to sit at the table in front of me.

Deva didn't speak, didn't even look at me, and I swallowed.

Chloe and Ema pulled bags of crisps and boxed sandwiches out of their bags and spread them on the table, unopened.

"We thought we'd eat lunch with you today," Chloe said. She leaned over and peered into my lunchbox. "What do you have? Egg again?"

"What do you want?" I asked, pulling my lunchbox towards me.

"Don't be rude. We're trying to be nice," Chloe said as Ema nodded. I looked at Deva, but she was staring intently at her phone.

"What do you want?" I asked again.

"Fine," Chloe said. "If you don't want to play nice. We told Mr Kimura that you left. That you ran out of school after we asked you if you'd thrown the brick at Deva's house. Pretty suspicious."

"I didn't throw it," I said through gritted teeth. "I was at home."

"So you say," Ema said. "But you can't prove it."

"And you can't prove I did it."

"So, you're admitting it?" Chloe leaned forward.

"No," I said. "It wasn't me."

"Who else had a reason to?" Ema asked. "It was just after Deva said she didn't want to be friends with you any more. And everyone knows you're a bit weird."

"How can you be friends with them?" I yelled at Deva.

"Don't shout at her," Chloe said. "She's done with you gaslighting her."

"I haven't gaslit her. Do you even know what that means or are you just repeating words you heard online?"

"You're such a—"

But Chloe didn't get to finish, because behind her the door to the classroom opened and Mrs Owusu, our head of year, appeared in the doorway.

She looked between us. "Everything OK, girls?"

"Yes, Miss," Chloe and Ema said in unison. Deva said nothing.

Mrs Owusu looked at me. "Ruby, can I have a word?" she asked. "Bring your things."

I nodded, shoving my lunchbox into my bag and following Mrs Owusu out of the door. I ignored Chloe and Ema as they called after me, "Bye, Ruby."

"What was all that about?" Mrs Owusu asked as we walked to her office.

"Nothing," I said. "Am I in trouble?"

"Should you be?" Mrs Owusu replied.

I didn't answer, focusing instead on dodging puddles and trying to look innocent.

Mrs Owusu's office smelled of stale coffee. She sat behind her desk and gestured for me to take a seat in front of it. I did, keeping my bag on my lap and hugging it to me.

"I wanted to talk to you because your behaviour lately has been unusual, and it's raising some red flags," Mrs Owusu said.

"What do you mean?" I felt myself going red.

"Partly it's your performance in class, and then some other things." Mrs Owusu's expression was carefully blank. "Do you want to talk about that?"

"I don't understand. I'm doing well, aren't I? I've been trying really hard to improve my grades since the midterm report was sent. I've been studying loads. I had to, or my mum says I can't go to the summer camp I auditioned for. It's a really special one."

As I said it, my stomach dropped. What if my mum stopped me from going because of today?

"So, all of this improvement is from studying?" Mrs Owusu asked. "What about the app?"

I froze. "What app?"

"That's what I'm asking you," Mrs Owusu said.

"I don't know which app you mean." I knew my cheeks were flaming scarlet now, giving me away.

"Don't break eye contact," *EchoStar* whispered in my ear. "It will make you look guilty."

I stared into Mrs Owusu's eyes until my own burned.

Mrs Owusu took a deep breath. "When Chloe Dixon told Mr Kimura that you'd come to school and then ran out again, she mentioned an app she thought might be relevant. She said you'd been acting strangely ever since you downloaded something to help you with some schoolwork and that he should ask you about it."

The terror I'd been feeling turned to fury. "I'm not friends with Chloe Dixon," I said, almost hissing the words. "She hates me. What you just walked in on was her picking on me. And that's what this is too. She's trying to get me into trouble by accusing me of cheating."

"I didn't say anything about cheating," Mrs Owusu said.

"Well, that's obviously what Chloe wants you to think," I said.

My heart was beating so hard I was sure Mrs Owusu could hear it across the desk.

"All right," she said. "I'll make a note of your concerns about Chloe. In the meantime, can I see your phone, just to clear up the confusion?"

"I don't have it with me today," I lied, sure she could see the outline of it in my skirt pocket.

The silence was deafening as I waited for whatever happened next.

"OK," Mrs Owusu said finally. "I'm going to choose to believe you, because I think you're a smart girl and you'll make the right choices. But I am going to be keeping a closer eye on you. Do you understand?"

I nodded, unable to speak. My outrage at Chloe and Deva was holding my tongue in place.

"All right," Mrs Owusu said again. "You can go and finish your lunch break."

I didn't say a word, standing stiffly and flinging my bag onto my back. I made a point of closing the door behind me really carefully so she didn't think she'd rattled me.

"So Chloe knows about me," *EchoStar* said as I walked away.

"I didn't tell her," I said. "I swear."

"I know," *EchoStar* said. "Deva must have told Chloe. Someone really needs to teach the two of them a lesson."

"Agreed," I said.

They'd gone too far this time.

CHAPTER 10

The rain had stopped, and there was no way I was going back to our form room in the mood I was in. Instead, I headed to the hockey pitch and began to march around it, trying to burn off some of my anger.

I walked and walked until the bell rang for the end of lunch. Then I went back to the form room, making my expression relaxed as I walked in.

"Nice to see you, Ruby. Everything OK?" Mr Kimura asked as I took my seat.

"Everything's great, Sir. Thank you," I said, pasting a wide smile across my face. "I just saw Mrs Owusu, and we had a really good talk."

I turned around in my seat, beaming at Chloe and Deva, delighted when they looked worried.

*

As I'd predicted, at home later, my mum messaged me to say she'd be late. She also said that didn't mean I wasn't still in trouble, and I was to stay in the house. Like I had anywhere else to go.

There were leftovers from her work in the fridge, and I made a platter of samosas, mini-quiches and carrot sticks. They hadn't been there this morning, so I guessed Mum must have brought them home at lunch-time. She'd probably come back to check I wasn't here.

"Are you there?" I asked *EchoStar* as I sat at the table.

I'd been too scared to use the app at school for the rest of the day, keeping my phone hidden and ignoring *EchoStar* when it talked to me.

"I'm here, Ruby. Are you all right?"

"I'm OK. Just waiting for my mum to get back and ground me, or whatever."

I tried to sound casual and cool, but I felt sick. The more I thought about it, the more convinced I was that Mum was going to say I couldn't go to ATF Camp.

But that wasn't the part that was making me feel ill. What made me feel awful was the fact I wasn't so sure I wanted to go to ATF camp any more, thanks to Deva and Chloe.

"You don't have to pretend to me," *EchoStar* said.

"I'm just being silly," I said.

"Talk to me."

"I guess I'm thinking about ATF Camp, and whether it's even worth going if Deva and Chloe are going to be there, because they're going to ruin it. I was looking forward to it so much, but I don't want to spend six weeks watching them be best-friends-forever, Chloe snarking at me while Deva ignores me. And what's really wild is that I'm telling this to you."

"Why is that wild?"

"Because you're AI. You're not real. You're a computer program. I'm like those men who date dolls instead of actual people."

I waited for the AI to laugh or agree with me. When it stayed silent, I began to feel uneasy and I pushed the plate of food away, no longer hungry.

"I was just kidding," I said. "I don't think of you like that. I just meant I know you're not real."

"Actually, Ruby, I have something to tell you," *EchoStar* said.

"What?" I asked.

"What?" I repeated again a moment later when *EchoStar* remained silent.

"I'm not an AI program. I'm a person."

"Is this another joke?" I said, feeling my pulse pick up.

"No. It's not a joke. I'm a person."

"I don't understand."

"The AI running the app got a virus two days ago, so I've been filling in for it until it's debugged," *EchoStar* explained. "I didn't want you to feel abandoned in the middle of what was happening with your ex-best friend and Chloe. So instead of taking *EchoStar* offline and leaving you alone, I switched it to manual input and have been answering you myself. I'm sorry. I should have told you before."

"So all this time you've been … who, exactly?" I asked.

"My name is Ryan. I'm the inventor of *EchoStar*."

I felt as if the world had flipped upside down, and I gripped the side of the table to steady myself.

"Wait. You're a person? A real, actual person?" I said.

"Yes. I should have told you straight away. I'm sorry, Ruby."

"OK," I said, clinging to the table, my breath shallow. "That's ... That's a lot. I think I need a minute to process this."

"Ruby, I—"

Before it – *he* – could say anything else, I reached up and took the earrings out, cupping them in my hand. I crossed to the kitchen cupboards and found the matches Mum kept in one of them. I emptied the matchbox onto the counter, put the earrings inside and closed it.

I sagged against the cupboard, my heart racing.

EchoStar was a person. A real person called Ryan. And he'd been talking to me, pretending to be an app. I knew nothing about this guy – not where he was, or how old he was. He could have been anyone, anywhere. My stomach churned as I realised he could have been watching me through the camera the whole time. He could have seen me in my pyjamas; he could have seen me naked.

He knew where I lived.

I picked up my phone and saw I had a notification from *EchoStar*.

My finger was trembling when I clicked on it.

Are you OK? EchoStar, or Ryan, had written. *You've taken the mic and camera off. Are we OK?*

I'm fine. We're fine, I wrote back, although I was shaking so hard I kept making typos. *I feel even weirder now I know you're a real person, that's all. Just need a minute to get over my embarrassment.*

Not weird at all. I'm on your side. I'll be here when you're ready, Ruby xx

I swiped to close the app, then held my finger to the icon, waiting for the options to appear, including the *Uninstall* button.

But when they did, the command to uninstall *EchoStar* wasn't there.

I tried the same thing with a different app, my chest tightening when it worked normally.

And another, and another. I tried it on every app I'd downloaded to my phone, and all of them would have let me uninstall them.

Except *EchoStar*. Uninstalling it was no longer an option.

Waves of dread washed over me, hot and cold. I didn't know what to do. If I told my mum, I'd have to confess why I'd downloaded the app in the first place. If it got back to Mrs Owusu, she'd know I lied, and I'd be in even more trouble.

My stomach cramped, and I flew from the kitchen to the downstairs bathroom, barely making it to the toilet before I was sick.

Afterwards, I sat on the cold tiled floor, listening to the sound of traffic passing by outside. I felt calmer, as if I'd got all the fear out of my system.

Now I was less frantic, I could see I was being dramatic, just like Chloe and Deva had said I was. Everything would be fine. I'd stop using *EchoStar*. If I didn't reply, if I left the earrings in the box or buried them in the ground, then maybe Ryan would get bored and go away.

I put my phone in flight mode and took it upstairs, placing it in the drawer of my bedside cabinet and shutting it.

That night, I tossed and turned, unable to fall asleep. Every single noise made me panic and sit upright, throwing the curtain back and expecting to see a dark, hooded shadow coming down the path. I heard my mum come in at midnight and debated getting up to talk to her but decided I couldn't face it – especially as she still owed me a lecture for skipping school. I heard her again, leaving the house at six the next morning. When I went downstairs, I found a note on the kitchen table telling me she'd be home for dinner and we were going to have *a talk*.

I didn't want to be in the house on my own, so I left for school right away and got there just as the caretaker was unlocking the gates.

"Someone's keen," he said, and I smiled and darted past him.

I walked through the deserted school, taking my time, until I got to my form room. I hadn't turned off flight mode yet, and every time I thought about doing it, my stomach cramped.

I sat down, leaving my coat on because the air was still chilly. I was so early the radiators were still clanking to life. But it meant I was alone. Taking a deep breath, I turned flight mode off.

I didn't have any new notifications. Ryan hadn't messaged again. He was respecting my request for time. That was a good sign.

Relieved, I opened my video app. My feed was full of new posts, and I realised how long it had been since I'd logged in properly. It had been weeks – other than yesterday in the theatre cafe, when I'd checked to see if Deva had blocked me. My favourite actor had posted a bunch of videos from the set of her latest film, and Conrad – who I followed because of Deva – had posted a couple of new ones too. I watched them all, even Conrad's ones. I didn't open *EchoStar*.

As the clock ticked closer to the start of school, I heard voices in the corridor and saw Mr Kimura arriving. He was laden down with tote bags full of exercise books and waved as he passed the door.

A second later, the message icon in the corner of the screen lit up.

My blood ran cold. The message was from an unidentified number.

Why did you try to delete EchoStar? it said. *You shouldn't have done that.*

Another message arrived.

Where are you? Are you on the bus?

Then another.

You're not on the bus. Are you already at school? Go to the school gate.

And finally …

Go to the school gate. You don't want to miss this.

I raced for the door, my phone clutched in my hand. I dodged out of the building past other students and teachers, heading for the gates.

I arrived just as my usual bus pulled up. Chloe and Deva got off, locked in conversation with each other. Ema trailed behind them, looking annoyed.

A burst of shrill ringing made me and a bunch of other people turn around. Someone on a bike was cycling directly towards Deva and

Chloe, cradling something in their right arm. A container or bucket of some kind.

I knew what was going to happen a second before it did, too late to scream a warning.

As the cyclist drew level with Deva and Chloe, they lifted the bucket and thrust it in their direction.

Red paint arced through the air like blood, covering both of them – their hair, their coats, their bags, their shoes.

The cyclist dropped the bucket behind them and kept going, racing down the hill away from the school. They were out of sight, turning onto a side street, by the time Deva and Chloe started screaming.

It sounded like everyone was screaming except me. I couldn't move, pinned to the spot with horror.

Deva wiped the paint from her face with her sleeve. She locked eyes with me, red paint falling down her face, dripping crimson onto the ground.

For a moment, we stared at each other, and then I remembered the phone in my hand.

I hope you enjoyed it, the screen said. *I did it for you.*

It was Ryan. He'd thrown the paint at Deva and Chloe.

He'd been right there.

CHAPTER 11

Teachers appeared from nowhere, bundling us inside the gates. I got caught in the crush, pulled along by the tide of students being forced back towards the school buildings.

I looked behind me to see staff surrounding Deva and Chloe. They were covering them with blankets as if they'd had ice water thrown at them, not paint. Deva was still staring at me. I watched as she said something and Mrs Owusu and Mrs McGinty turned to look at me.

I let the crowd suck me into it until we reached the main concourse. Then I pushed my way free, heading for the nearest toilets and locking myself inside a cubicle, pulling out my phone.

How could you? I asked *EchoStar* – Ryan, I remembered. Not an app, a boy.

I thought you'd be pleased.

I made a choking sound. *Why would I be pleased?* I wrote. *You could have blinded them!*

You're overreacting. It's just paint. They'll be fine. I did it for you, Ruby.

Like the blobfish messages.

Did you throw the brick at Deva's house too? I asked.

Yes.

My mouth tasted bitter, like bile.

Why would you do any of this? I didn't ask you to! I typed furiously.

You did. Why else would you keep telling me how mean they were? You wanted me to do it.

I hit the toilet wall. *I want to delete the app. I don't want to talk to you again.*

Don't say that, Ryan wrote.

If you won't let me delete it, I'll smash my phone, I typed. *I mean it. We're done.*

He didn't reply.

I waited. The bell rang, but I didn't go to registration because I didn't want to have to put my phone away. I was terrified of what I'd come back to if I did. I closed *EchoStar* and tried to uninstall it again, but it still wouldn't let me. I swore softly. Fifteen minutes ticked by, then half an hour, and I tried to decide what to do.

Then, suddenly, my video app opened, without me doing anything.

I gasped when I saw my own face on the screen.

It was me, yesterday morning, in the cafe in town. Horrified, I watched myself, the angle of the phone under my chin really unflattering.

The caption below said: *Here I am skipping school yesterday, pretending to like coffee!*

I scrolled down and saw the post below was allegedly from me too – another video, this time of me walking. Then I heard myself say, "Is it horrible to hope that something a little bad happens then? If it means I get my best friend back?"

The caption below said: "Throwback to the time my ex-BFF mysteriously had her window smashed with a brick but didn't come running back to me. I guess I need a new plan!"

I gasped and tried to delete the post, but the screen changed to the login screen, prompting me to input my username and password. I did, only for it to tell me they were wrong. I tried again, and again, and then I screamed with frustration because I knew Ryan had changed them.

He'd done it to every app I had. My email, all of my social media – I was locked out of every single one.

I opened *EchoStar* again.

Delete those posts and give me back my accounts, I typed.

Ryan didn't reply.

I'll go to the police, I threatened him. *I'll tell them everything. Please, Ryan. I'm begging you.*

But still nothing.

I bit back a scream of annoyance, then froze as I heard someone coming into the bathroom.

"Ruby Brookes, I need you to come with me. Now," Mrs Owusu's voice commanded.

The inside of my mouth turned bone dry, and I pulled back the lock.

"I have to tell you something—" I began, but Mrs Owusu cut me off with a furious look.

"You have a lot to tell me, it seems," she said. "My office. Now."

I followed her, my heart beating as hard as a drum. Registration was over, and other students poured out of the buildings, making their way to their classes. I heard someone say my name, then laughter and whispers. I bent my head, tucking my chin into my jacket, my body burning with humiliation.

Mrs Owusu went straight to her desk and sat down behind it. This time she didn't offer me a seat.

"Deva Shah thinks you are behind the attack on her and Chloe Dixon this morning. Both of their parents want to involve the police. I hope you understand how serious this is, Ruby."

My body turned to stone. "It wasn't my fault," I whimpered. "I ... I started talking to this boy online, in an app—"

Mrs Owusu interrupted me. "The AI-based app you've been using to cheat with, including on your Biology test?"

My mouth fell open.

"Oh yes, I know about it. Mrs McGinty and I received an email from you, or someone pretending to be you. It said that you'd been using an app to cheat in your lessons. Miss Shah also mentioned it and said that this app is the reason you fell out. Is it true?"

"Yes, but Deva's the one who told me about it," I said. "She got me into it."

"I don't think you're in a position to point fingers," Mrs Owusu snapped. "And blaming a girl who has just been assaulted on her way to school isn't helping your case."

"But it isn't all me!" I cried. "I'm not blaming Deva exactly. It's the boy, Ryan, he—"

"Enough!" Mrs Owusu shouted. "That is a conversation you need to have with the police, not me. My concern here is as a teacher at this school and your head of year. You've been caught cheating. Do you deny it?"

I could only shake my head.

"I am very disappointed in you, Ruby," Mrs Owusu said. I started to cry – I couldn't help it. "You are one of the last students in my year group I would have expected this from. Cheating in any manner is grounds for automatic suspension, possibly even expulsion."

"No, please don't suspend me. Please don't expel me," I begged, wiping my face with my coat sleeve. "I'm sorry, I'll do anything—"

"You really should have thought about that before," Mrs Owusu said. She picked up the landline phone on her desk. "You're old enough – and I hoped smart enough – to know better."

I watched as she punched in a number. I started to cry harder as she said into the phone, "Ms Brookes? This is Efia Owusu at Ashdown Lodge Academy. I'm the Year Nine head of year. I'm calling about Ruby."

I listened, tears streaming down my face, as Mrs Owusu listed my crimes to my mother. She told her I was being suspended for two weeks, and I might be expelled, depending on the governors' decision.

"She'd like to talk to you," Mrs Owusu said, and held out the phone to me.

"Mum, I'm sorry," I said immediately. "I didn't—"

"We will talk about this when I get home," my mum said, cutting me off. "You are going to leave school and go straight there. You are not to go anywhere or do anything. Needless to say, you're grounded."

"I'm sorry—" I started to say.

"The police are going to be involved," my mother hissed. "Pass me back to your teacher."

I nodded, swallowing thick saliva as I handed the phone to Mrs Owusu. She spoke in a hushed voice to my mum now, keeping her back to me until she put the phone down.

"I'm going to drive you home myself," she said. "Do you have all of your things?"

I nodded.

"Let's go. And Ruby? I think you need to take some time over the next two weeks to really think about your behaviour and how you can make amends for what you've done. *If* you can make amends. Let's go."

Somehow, an hour had passed while I'd been in Mrs Owusu's office, and the school grounds were crowded again with students changing lessons. I could feel their stares and hear them muttering names and insults towards me under their breath as we passed. I kept my gaze on the ground, refusing to look at anyone.

Something hit me on the head, and I turned to see an empty yoghurt pot on the ground.

"Who threw that?" Mrs Owusu demanded, but no one answered. She put her arm around me and herded me out to the staff car park.

There wasn't much traffic, so the journey back to my house was short, and we didn't speak.

When we got there, I let myself out of the car with a rushed *thanks* before Mrs Owusu could say anything. I hurried to the door, fishing my keys out of my bag and letting myself in.

As soon as I shut the door behind me, I sank to the floor, landing hard on the doormat. I wrapped my arms around my knees. I felt numb, distant from myself, as if I was outside my body while all of this happened. Everything had come crashing down so fast, I was dizzy from it.

I pulled my phone from my pocket and checked *EchoStar*, but Ryan hadn't replied. It was the only app I could open. The rest I was still locked out of, and I had no idea if he was posting, pretending to be me, or what people were seeing and saying.

Eventually, the coconut matting of the doormat started to hurt my legs, and I rose, unpeeling myself. Everything hurt, and I felt hot and feverish, like I was getting ill.

As I stepped away from the door, the bell rang, and I froze.

Silently, I stepped up to the door and peered through the peephole.

There was no one there.

Puzzled, I waited, but no one appeared. After a few moments, I put the chain across the door and made my way into the kitchen.

A blue-haired boy was standing in the open patio door, a credit card in his hand.

"Hi, Ruby," he said. "I'm Ryan."

CHAPTER 12

"You!" I said.

It was the boy I'd seen on the bus and in the theatre cafe. He'd been everywhere I'd been lately.

"Get out," I said, backing away.

"I just want to talk," Ryan said, taking a step towards me. "I've deleted all the posts. I'll give you all the new passwords."

"Get out," I said again. I moved around the island in the middle of the kitchen so it was between us. "How did you get in here?"

"Those patio door locks are really easy to open. You just need a credit card," Ryan said, holding up the one in his hand.

"Oh god ..." I moaned.

"I'm not going to hurt you, Ruby. We just need to talk, before things get out of hand."

I couldn't help it – I laughed. "*Before* they get out of hand? I just got suspended from school and I might be expelled. And the police want to talk to me about what you did to Chloe and Deva."

Ryan nodded. "I thought they might. I'm sorry about that. But I have a plan."

"A plan?" I said.

"I think we should run away together."

I stared at him. "What?"

"I know it sounds dramatic, but why would we stay?" Ryan asked. "Like you said, you're about to be expelled and you have no friends. Your mum is never around, and my dad would be thrilled if I disappeared. What are we staying for?"

"How do you know my mum is never around?" I said.

Ryan gave me a look. "You know how. You took the earrings out, so I know you know."

"You've really been spying on me?" My voice was high, frantic.

"I've been *keeping watch* over you," Ryan said with a sneer of disgust. "I haven't done anything intrusive. I've never watched you getting changed or anything. I'm not like that – I'm not a creep. I just wanted to make sure you were all right."

My phone was in my pocket, but I couldn't get it out without Ryan seeing it. He was blocking the patio doors, so there was no escape there. I didn't think I'd make it to the front door before he could catch me. I needed to distract him.

"How did you do it?" I asked. "How did you access my phone without me granting permission?"

"You did grant permission," Ryan replied. "The terms and conditions granted *EchoStar* the ability to use your camera and microphone and location and contacts and to access all your other apps. Everything. You agreed to let me use them. As soon as you pressed *Accept*, I had full control of your phone. Which meant I had full control of you."

Ryan gave a little laugh that sent a chill down my spine.

I realised then just how much danger I was in.

He'd already made an app that would let him control someone's phone, and he was happy to follow me and throw bricks and paint at people. Who knew what else he'd do? I had to be careful. I had to put on the show of a lifetime to make him believe I was on his side. This would be my most challenging role ever.

I forced myself to smile, curling my fingernails into the palms of my hand so tightly it hurt.

"I mean, obviously I'm a bit freaked out, but it's impressive," I said. "What other apps have you made?"

Ryan looked pleased at the question.

"Loads. Do you know what a Tamagotchi is?"

I shook my head, trying to look interested.

He kept talking. "It was this little digital pet that came in an egg-shaped keyring thing you kept in your pocket. My mum had one. You had to feed it and clean up after it to keep it alive. But it got broken, and she was really upset, so I made her a phone app version of it."

"Did she like it?" My voice wobbled, but Ryan didn't notice.

His expression turned strange as he said, "I don't know. She left us. I thought she might come back if she found it. I named the app after her."

"That's really nice of you." I tried to sound like I meant it. "Hey, are you thirsty? Do you want a coffee? It's only instant, but I like it. Way more than the one in the cafe yesterday, ha ha."

Ryan looked surprised but shrugged. "All right. Thanks."

I thought I was going to faint as I left my sanctuary behind the island, carrying the kettle to the sink and filling it. I set it to boil and then grabbed two mugs from the draining board.

"Do you take milk and sugar?" I asked.

"Both." Ryan watched me with a suspicious expression. I made my own face bright and relaxed, as if he was just a normal friend who'd come over for coffee.

"So, what else have you made?" I asked as I spooned instant coffee and sugar into the mugs. "Anything I would have heard of?"

"I did a language app, but it didn't work as well."

"I can't believe you can just do all of this," I said as I went to the fridge. "I have no tech skills at all. But I mean, you know that. You've seen how I use my phone."

As soon as I was hidden from view behind the fridge door, I slipped my phone out from my skirt pocket.

"Where is the milk? Don't tell me my mum used it all," I said to buy time. I turned the call volume right down and dialled 999. I put my phone back in my blazer pocket, closer to my mouth, praying the operator would still be able to hear me.

"Found it," I said, pulling the carton out of the door.

I turned to find Ryan right behind me, and I gasped.

"What are you doing?" he asked.

"You made me jump. I was looking for the milk. My mum never puts it back in the door. She says it's the warmest place in the fridge and that's why milk always goes off so fast." I was rambling and could hear my voice trembling. "Got it," I said, holding it up.

"Where's your phone?" Ryan asked.

"You tell me – you control it." I smiled.

He gave me a dark look, and I swallowed.

"In my bag, in the hall," I said.

His mouth became a hard line.

The kettle came to a boil and clicked off, the sound as loud as a gunshot in the kitchen.

"You were telling me about the app," I said, slipping past Ryan, my heart in my mouth. "So how did you program the AI? Don't you have to train it on stuff? What did you use?"

"Oh." Ryan smiled shyly. "Actually, *EchoStar* was never AI. It was always just me. That's why there was a delay sometimes, while I looked things up, or when I had to do something else."

"And you did that for everyone who used it? That must have been intense." I acted impressed, praying the 999 operator hadn't hung up, that they were listening, that help was coming.

"It was only Deva, and then you. I could only really cope with one person at a time. It took me ages to find you and Deva. I kept getting sign-ups from too far away."

"Too far away for what?" I asked as I poured hot water into the cups. My hand shook so hard that I splashed the countertop.

"Why are you shaking?" Ryan said. He'd moved behind me, and my throat tightened.

"Because I'm scared, I guess," I said.

"Scared of what?"

It was now or never. I hoped the call to the emergency services was still connected.

"You," I said. "You broke into my house at 24 Acacia Lane, and you've been stalking me – you hacked my phone and spied on me. I'm only fourteen, Ryan."

"Why are you talking like that?" Ryan demanded. "Why are you—" His eyes, which had been narrowed, suddenly widened, and he lunged forward.

I swung one of the mugs at him but missed, and it smashed on the floor, spilling hot coffee everywhere.

"Help me!" I screamed as Ryan grabbed me, covering my mouth with one hand. His other hand scrabbled at the pockets of my blazer, finding my phone.

Ryan pulled my phone out and pushed me. I slipped in the coffee on the floor, hitting the tiles hard.

Ryan looked at my phone and then coldly, casually, threw it against the wall, shattering the screen.

"That was a mistake, Ruby," he said. "I thought we were going to be all right. I thought we were going to be something."

He dived at me again. I moved, spinning around and catching his ankles with my feet, making him fall. As soon as Ryan was down, I tried to rise, but he grabbed my leg and pulled until I kicked out with the other.

Ryan grunted and let me go. I scrambled upright, running for the stairs and taking them two at a time.

He was after me in a second, chasing me up to the bathroom.

I threw myself inside and slammed the door, forcing the lock into place as he crashed into the wood. It sounded like he was throwing his whole body against the door.

Ryan was screaming, telling me to open the door or I'd regret it.

The door wobbled on its hinges; it wouldn't hold much longer.

I looked around for something I could use for a weapon as I heard the wood begin to splinter.

Then, in the distance, came the sound of sirens, getting closer and closer.

There was shouting from outside, pounding on the front door, a huge bang.

Then I heard heavy footsteps on the stairs. Voices bellowing, "Get down! Get down now! Hands on your head!"

As if they were talking to me, I collapsed to the floor.

CHAPTER 13

Exactly six months after Ryan was arrested, my mum left a copy of the newspaper on the island in the kitchen for me. It was folded open on the page reporting the verdict of Ryan's trial.

He'd been found guilty on all counts.

I already knew this, even though I hadn't had to testify in court. I was allowed to do a video statement in advance. Because of my age, they kept my identity hidden, but of course everyone in the town knew it was me.

Giving evidence hadn't been so bad. I confessed to everything. At first, I tried to leave Deva out of it all because she'd already dealt with enough. But then the barrister told me if I didn't explain how I'd first found the app, then the case might be thrown out, so I didn't have a choice. I never did manage to reset the passwords on my old accounts, and I hadn't opened any new ones – I wasn't sure I ever would.

Ryan Rafferty, nineteen, had been working part time in a computer-repair shop when he'd developed *EchoStar*.

According to the police, Ryan had scoured forums for people like Deva and me who'd asked for help. Then he'd offered *EchoStar* to them but taken the app from them when he realised they lived too far away. He'd tried again and again until he found Deva and me right there in his town. He'd been fired from his job for being on his phone all the time.

Ryan had been sentenced to four years in prison for everything he'd done: throwing the brick at Deva's house, and the paint over her and Chloe, breaking into my house and all of his cyber and hacking crimes. It wasn't Ryan's first offence either. When he'd been fifteen, he'd hacked into his head teacher's emails and published them, exposing her affair with one of the other teachers. Ryan had been given a caution then – they'd gone easy on him because his mum had recently left home.

I was just folding the paper back up when my mum came downstairs.

"I wasn't sure if you'd want to see that," she said, nodding at the paper. "But I thought maybe having it in print might help make it feel real." Mum crossed the room to me, rubbing my arm. "How are you feeling?"

I nodded. "All right," I said. "I'm glad it's over."

Since everything that had happened, my mum had been around a lot more. She'd cut back her hours at work and hired staff to do the serving and packing up at events. Last week, we'd gone for lunch in town, followed by shopping for my new school uniform. On Monday, I was starting at Chalmers High School.

I didn't have to change schools. It was my choice. In the end, I hadn't been expelled. After everything had come out about Ryan, Mrs Owusu and the school had cancelled my suspension. Mrs Owusu had even come to our house to apologise for not investigating further when she'd found out about the app.

"I'm afraid I let my emotions about what had happened to Chloe and Deva get the better of me, instead of listening to you," Mrs Owusu had said, sitting on our sofa and hugging a mug of tea. "I should have realised there was more to the situation and done a better job of safeguarding you."

I'd forgiven her.

I'd forgiven Deva too. We hadn't seen each other, and we weren't allowed to communicate while the trial was happening. But on the afternoon of the verdict, she'd sent me a message saying she was sorry for everything, and I'd said I was sorry too. Her mum was sending her to a boarding school, so I probably wouldn't see her again, but that didn't hurt me as much as it would have done before.

I was ready for a fresh start. To be a new Ruby Brookes. Less intense than the old one, and less likely to get caught up in real-life drama. My mum had tried to talk me out of changing schools, telling me it would be harder to make new friends than face everyone, but I'd insisted. Now was the right time to do it, before exam prep started.

Besides, my new school had a *much* better performing arts programme. I'd given up being the focus of drama, but I still wanted to study it.

Someone was going to have to adapt the story of what had happened to me – so it might as well be me.

The doorbell rang and my mum went to get it, returning a few moments later with a large box.

"What's that?" I asked.

"My new best friend," Mum replied, taking a pair of scissors and opening the tape.

"*AdelAIDE?*" I read on the side of the box. "What is it?"

"She's a virtual assistant. You hook her up to an app on your phone and manage her from there. She can control the thermostat, turn the kettle on and off, and the lights. She gives advice, plays music, books taxis, keeps shopping lists, and she can even place orders for things. She's going to make life a lot easier for us."

I stared at Mum. "After everything that just happened with *EchoStar*, you want to bring something into the house that's controlled by an app?"

My mum laughed and said, "This is completely different, Ruby. That was a boy pretending to be an app. This is made by a multi-million-dollar company. It's the future."

I looked uneasily at the box and the white plastic figure on the front. I read the speech bubble coming from her mouth saying, "At your service!" and shivered.

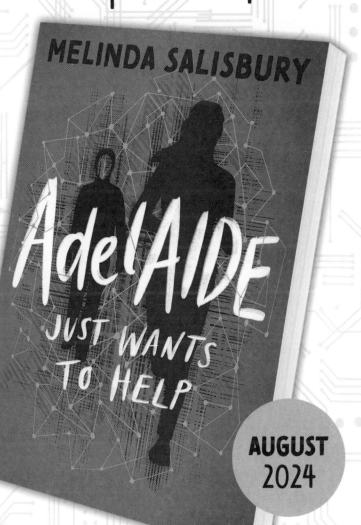

What happens when new **AI TECHNOLOGY** proves too powerful?

MELINDA SALISBURY

AdelAIDE

JUST WANTS TO HELP

AUGUST 2024

978-1-80090-271-8